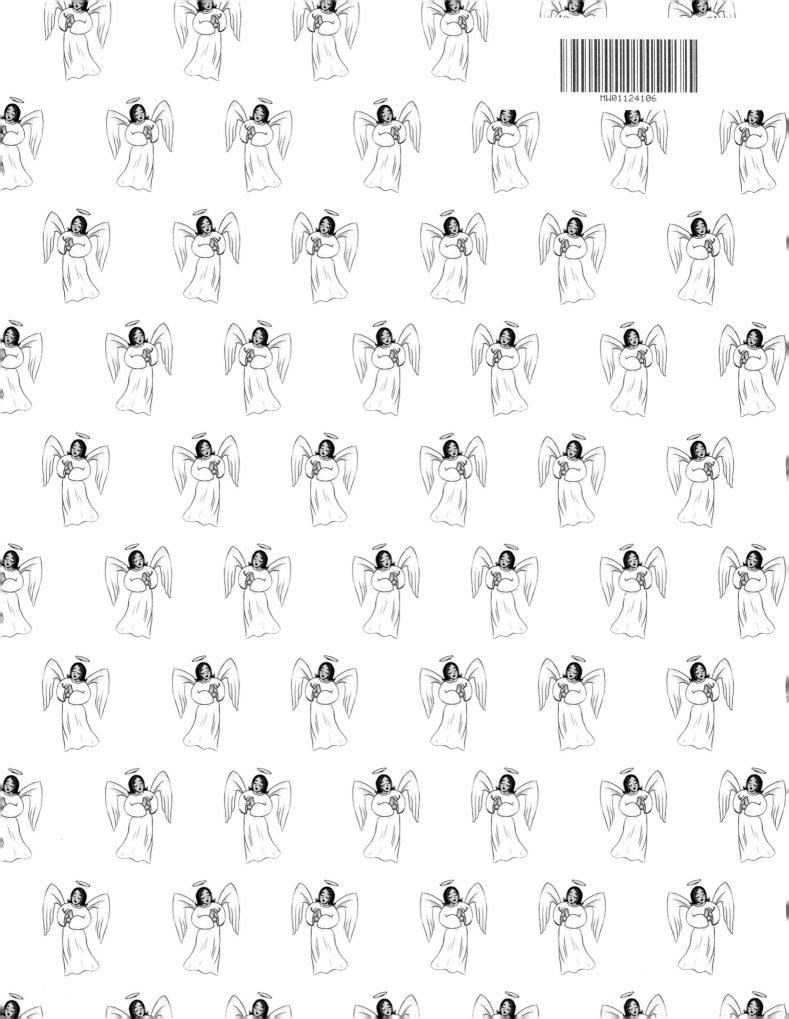

Dedicated to my dad, Norman,
of whom I have memories
of amusement and admonition,
but mostly adoration.
Dad was a proud man with a tender heart.

The Tale of Norman the Nutcracker and the Sour Pickle by Rosa Veenstra.
Published by Zonneschijn Publishing

ISBN-13 978-0-692-10333-3

Text by Rosa Veenstra
Illustrations by Kristna Vukmirovic

THE TALE OF
NORMAN THE NUTCRACKER
AND THE SOUR PICKLE

A Story from the Christmas Tree

by Rosa Veenstra

All of the ornaments
were restless with excitement
because it was Christmas Eve.

GLORY, GLORY, GLORY, TO GOD

The angels were practicing their singing for the midnight carol.

The lights were twinkling,
the glittery ornaments were glittering,
and the tinsel was sparkling.

And under the tree stood the Nutcracker tall and proud.

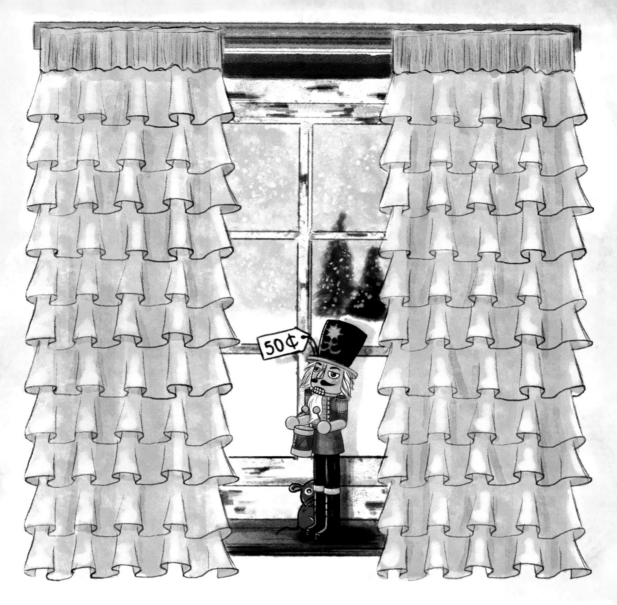

The couple purchased the wooden Nutcracker many years ago from the thrift store for fifty cents. He was their first Christmas decoration. They brought him home and set him on the windowsill, very happy with their purchase. They called him Norman because the name suited the tall, proud Nutcracker.

Over the years the family grew and collected more Christmas decorations. Norman's place moved from the windowsill to the base of the tree.

When the boy was two, he carried Norman around like he was a toy. He wanted to take Norman to bed with him, but Mommy said, "No, Norman must keep watch by the tree." That upset the boy so much that he threw Norman on the floor.

After Mommy put the boy to bed, she noticed that Norman had a chip on his hat from the boy's tantrum.

So each Christmas Norman kept watch by the tree. He took his job very seriously. He made sure the lights twinkled, the glittery ornaments glittered, the tinsel sparkled, and Piet the Pickle hid.

Piet the glass pickle ornament, was a gift to the family and it became a tradition to hide the pickle in the tree on Christmas Eve. The next morning, the first one to find the pickle would get to open the first gift.

On this Christmas Eve, the children were finally asleep in their beds. Norman watched as the father tiptoed into the living room and peered into the tree. All the ornaments held their breath as he reached into the tree and hung the pickle on a low branch inside near the trunk. The father smiled, as if pleased, and tiptoed off to bed.

Everyone let out a collective sigh when the bedroom door clicked shut. It was almost time for the midnight angel chorus.

GLORY IN THE HIGHEST

At last the clock on the mantle struck twelve. The angels started singing the beautiful chorus.

♫ GLORY, GLORY, GLORY, TO GOD ♫

At first, none of the ornaments paid any attention to the miserable wailing coming from a low branch near the trunk of the tree. But as the angels got louder, so did the sour sounds. It was awful!

GRUMBLE

MOAN

UGH

GRUNT

GROAN

The best part of Christmas was being ruined by a sour pickle! It sounded so terrible that the angels stopped singing. The other ornaments were so disappointed that the pickle was ruining Christmas. They started yelling at the pickle and calling him names.

Norman just stood there. Soon a tear slipped down his cheek, then another. This was not the way Christmas is supposed to be. The joy and peace had turned into anger and chaos. One by one, the lights, the ornaments, the tinsel, the angels, and Piet noticed Norman's tears. They all became silent and were embarrassed by their behavior.

"Piet," Norman asked,
"Why are you having a tantrum and
spoiling the angels' song?"
Piet replied, "I'm mad that everyone
else get to twinkle, glitter and sparkle
all season long and I only get to
participate one night. It isn't fair!"

Norman thought about what Piet said. At last, he began to speak quietly at first, then more confidently. "My heart hurts because all of you forgot the meaning of this night. We are here to celebrate Jesus' birth. Christmas is not about us. It is not about what we do or what we give or get. It is not about how much time we get to spend in the tree. It is about loving others the way we are loved by God who sent His Son to be born on Christmas."

He continued, "That is why angels sing, lights twinkle, glittery ornaments glitter, tinsel sparkles, and the pickle hides. That's why God created us. We are each here for a special purpose and we each have a task we are made to do. Sometimes our job seems small or unimportant, but God is pleased when we do our jobs without complaining."

GLORY, GLORY, GLORY, TO GOD

One by one, the angels
started to sing again,
"Glory, Glory, Glory to God,
Glory in the Highest!"

GLORY IN THE HIGHEST

The lights started to shine, the glittery ornaments glittered, the tinsel sparkled, and even the pickle changed his sour expression to a sweet one.

Everyone got excited for Christmas morning when the family would gather around the tree for their celebration of the birth of Jesus. Norman stood tall and proud keeping watch by the tree. His heart was filled with joy.